D0257325

The Wonder
on the Forth

First published in 1999 by
SCOTTISH CHILDREN'S PRESS
Unit 13c, Newbattle Abbey Business Centre,
Newbattle Road, Dalkeith EH22 3LJ
e-mail: scp@sol.co.uk
http://www.taynet.co.uk/users/scp

© Donald Lightwood, 1999

the right of Donald Lightwood to be identified as the Author of
this Work has been asserted by him in accordance with the
Copyright, Designs and Patents Act, 1988

*All rights reserved. No part of this publication may be reproduced,
stored in a retrieval system, or transmitted in any form or by any means,
electronic, mechanical, photocopying, recording or otherwise without the prior
permission, in writing, of Scottish Children's Press*

The publisher acknowledges subsidy from

towards the publication of this volume

British Library Cataloguing in Publication Data
A catalogue record for this book is available from the British Library

ISBN: 1 899827 92 7

Cover illustration by Alexa Rutherford
Cover design by Craig Ellery
Printed and bound by Colour Books Ltd, Dublin

The Wonder on the Forth

9010016565

DONALD LIGHTWOOD

SCOTTISH CHILDREN'S PRESS

To David, Jenny and Gavin,
who crossed the bridge to Fife

One

Morag and Alec looked for a way out of the playground, but they were trapped. The crowd of children moved closer and closer. They were shouting and pointing.

'Stinky tinks! Stinky tinks!'

'We're not tinkers!' Morag yelled back.

'Stinky tinks, live in a tent.' The chant went on.

Alec held his sister's hand. 'They always pick on us,' he said, frightened.

A lump of mud hit Morag. Alec picked up a stone and hurled it back blindly. There was a cry of pain from somebody.

'Stinky tinks, live in a tent.'

Some of the braver children ran out of the crowd to kick at Morag and Alec. Others spat at them.

Morag pushed over a boy who had lost his balance.

Alec spat at him.

There was uproar. It was as if their attackers had suddenly been insulted. They charged forward and Morag and Alec were crushed under a pile of bodies. But they weren't badly hurt. While they were wedged in a heap nobody could do much kicking or punching.

A whistle sounded. It was the dominie. He came marching out of the school carrying his tawse. Children scrambled to their feet, hoping to escape.

'Stand still,' he ordered. The playground froze.

Morag and Alec were on the ground. The dominie looked at them. 'You two again,' he said. 'Get up. You've been nothing but trouble since you came to North Queensferry.'

Standing in front of the schoolmaster in their ragged clothes and bare feet, they made a scruffy pair. Their noses were running and Alec was crying.

'They were calling us names,' said Morag.

'Sir,' corrected the dominie.

'They were calling us names, sir,' she repeated.

'I heard them.'

'We weren't doing nothing, sir,' she told him.

Alec sniffed and wiped his hand across his face. 'It was no' our fault,' he muttered.

The dominie regarded him with disgust. 'You two are here. That's what is at fault.'

'Please, sir, he threw a stone at me,' said one of the boys.

'He spat at me,' added another.

'Silence!' snapped the dominie. 'We have been cursed by incomers,' he went on. 'The building of this bridge may be a miracle of engineering, but it has brought dross in its wake. Ne'er-do-well labourers and their uncouth bairns. The village will never be the same again.'

'We always get the blame,' Morag mumbled.

Stung by her impertinence, the dominie shook his finger at her. 'Your father should be ashamed of himself. Look at the state of you. He has a wage. You're not paupers.'

'He's better than you!' Alec cried.

'Be quiet,' the dominie responded. 'I'll deal with you two later.' He called out to the rest of the children. 'Into a line. The lot of you.'

Knowing what was coming, there was pushing and shoving to be at the end of the line. The dominie's arm would be tired by the time he got there.

'Hands out!' he commanded, and set about belting each child's palm with his tawse.

Morag and Alec stood watching. Their tormentors' punishment gave them no pleasure. It would just be used as another reason to bully them.

'Now you two,' the dominie told them. 'Hands out.'

'They started it,' Morag replied.

'You were fighting in the yard. Hold out your hand.'

Morag looked up at the tall, black-clad figure glowering at her. He was breathing heavily and his face was covered with sweat. He knew it wasn't fair, punishing her and Alec. But he was going to do it, just because of who they were.

'No!' Morag shouted at him and grabbed her brother's hand. 'Come on, Alec.' She pulled him after her and they ran out of the playground and away from the school.

'He'll tell our father,' said Alec.

'No he'll no',' said Morag.

'He will so. And we'll get skelped and have to go to school, and get another skelping there as well.' Alec nibbled his nails anxiously.

'The dominie'll be glad to be rid of us. He'll no' say nothing.'

They were sitting on a bank overlooking the north road. It was busy with carts carrying wooden railway sleepers for the new bridge.

'I wish I was a horse,' said Alec, as the large carthorses lumbered by.

'For all you ken, they could be wishing they were you,' Morag told him. 'Sitting here, no' hoiking great loads around.'

Alec sat silently and then spoke. 'Why did our mother have to die?'

Morag sighed to herself. Sometimes she wished she wasn't Alec's older sister. She shook her head. 'I dinna ken.'

'Why are their mothers no' dead? At the school. They're pigs. Why did it have to be us?'

'She was ill.'

'It's no' right.'

Morag put her arm round his shoulders. 'It's no good fretting. You ken that. Just think, you'd be having to say your tables if we were in the school.'

'I wish that dominie was dead,' said Alec.

She shrugged. 'They'd just find another one.'

Suddenly a dog appeared in front of them. It was wagging its tail so hard, the whole of its body was shaking. Before they could speak it had jumped up and was licking their faces. They rolled on the grass laughing.

'Where did you come from?' cried Morag, rubbing the dog's shaggy coat.

'Here boy!' called Alec, getting up and running away. The dog charged after him. 'Fetch!' He sent the dog racing after a stick.

They played until the three of them were out of breath.

'Can we keep him?' said Alec, hugging the dog. 'I'm going to call him Rob, after Rob Roy.' He spoke into the dog's ear. 'You – Rob. Me – Alec.' The dog rubbed his snout on Alec's nose.

'He must belong to somebody,' said Morag.

'He wants to stay with us. You can tell.'

'Och, he'd only run away when it suited him.'

'Dinna you listen to her,' Alec told the dog.

Morag cocked her head up and looked along the road. She could hear the clip-clop of a coach horse and the jangling of harness. A smart hackney carriage came into view.

'Rob, come back!' Alec shouted. The dog had wriggled out of his arms and run down to the road. It began barking at the horse and snapping at its legs.

The coachman slashed at the dog with his whip.

'You stop that!' yelled Alec, as he and Morag slithered down the bank.

The coach halted and the coachman jumped off to calm the horse. The dog was growling and he gave it a hefty kick.

Alec ran at the man and threw himself at him. Cursing, the man tried to hit Alec with his whip.

With a shout, Morag grabbed at the whip with both hands and tugged it from the coachman's grip and threw it down. The horse reared to strike out at the dog with its hooves. The coach tilted backwards and there was a scream from inside. The man hung on to the horse's neck and the coach righted itself. The door swung open and a woman stepped out. She was extremely angry.

'What on earth is going on?' she demanded.

'Sorry ma'am, it's this dog,' called the coachman, still struggling with the horse.

'My daughter is terrified. Step out of the coach, Amelia.'

A girl of about Morag's age got out. Like her mother, she was dressed in a travelling coat with leg of mutton sleeves and a fur-trimmed hat. She pressed herself against her mother and hid her face.

'These two brats attacked me,' the coachman told the woman.

She regarded Morag and Alec sternly. 'Is this true?'

'He kicked my dog,' said Alec.

'And he whipped my brother,' cried Morag.

'So I should think,' retorted the woman. 'Allowing your dog to do such a thing. The animal should be shot.'

'No he shouldn't!' Alec shouted back at her.

'Dinna you answer your betters like that, or you'll feel my hand,' the coachman threatened him.

The woman wrinkled her nose, as if Morag and Alec were giving off a bad smell. 'We could have been seriously injured.'

Amelia peeped around her mother at Morag, her eyes wide at the sight of the other girl. Morag stuck her tongue out at her, and she hid her face again.

'What I should like to know is why you are here,' said the woman. 'You are both of an age to be at school. Well?'

Morag and Alec glanced at each other, but said nothing.

'You answer when the lady speaks to you,' said the coachman.

'I asked why you are not at school,' the woman repeated.

'We dinna have to go,' Alec mumbled.

Morag groaned to herself. She could have shaken him.

'All children have to go to school. If you do not, your parents will be prosecuted. It is the law. What are your names?'

The two remained silent.

The coachman spoke to the woman. 'From the look of them, they'll be navvy's bairns, ma'am.'

'Are you?' she demanded. 'Does your father work for the bridge company?'

Morag shrugged and nodded.

'Then it may interest you to know that my name is Mrs Wright and my husband is a Board of Trade Inspector for the bridge. Do you wish your father to get into trouble for breaking the law?'

Morag let out a cry. 'No, mistress. Dinna do that!'

'I shall have to see about that,' said Mrs Wright. 'Now, what are your names?' she asked. They told her. She clicked her tongue. 'Your mother should be ashamed of herself. Your clothes are disgusting. There is no excuse. Your father is earning a wage.'

'We haven't got no mother,' said Alec.

'She died afore we came here,' Morag added.

'I see.' Mrs Wright frowned. 'Where do you live?'

'In my father's tent,' said Morag.

'Huts have been erected for the labourers.'

'We canna afford one o' them,' Morag told her.

'Why not?'

Morag shrugged.

'As like as not, he'll be drinking his wages, ma'am,' said the coachman.

'Shut it, you!' cried Alec at the man.

'Undoubtedly,' said Mrs Wright. 'He is certainly not looking after his family.'

'Dinna blame my father,' said Morag in a worried voice. 'He has to be away at his work all day.'

'So does everyone else,' said Mrs Wright. 'That does not excuse him from his responsibilities.'

Amelia giggled. She had seen Alec step back into a muddy puddle, avoiding a clout from the coachman. His bare feet squelched in the mud.

'That will do, Amelia,' said her mother. 'Remember, they are less fortunate than you.'

'Their dog's run away,' said Amelia.

'Rob!' Alec shouted, but the dog had disappeared. He glared at Amelia, who wrinkled her nose just like her mother.

'Mistress, we'll go back to the school,' said Morag. 'Dinna say nothing, please. We're sorry about what the dog done.'

Mrs Wright looked down at her. 'I should hope you are.' Her haughty attitude softened slightly. 'I do not hold you entirely to blame. It's clear to me that you and your brother have been neglected. Something one expects in the slums of Glasgow, but certainly not here. My husband tells me there is work for everybody.'

'My father needs his job, and he's good to us,' Morag pleaded.

'Can we be on our way now?' Mrs Wright asked the coachman.

'Aye, ma'am. The horse's calmed down.'

'Very well. Apologise to this gentleman for the trouble you have caused,' she went on to Morag and Alec.

The two mumbled that they were sorry and Mrs Wright and Amelia got back into the coach. The girl pressed her face against the window, staring at the other children as if they were creatures from another world.

Morag and Alec watched the coach go down the road.

'Why's she no' at school?' said Alec.

'They're rich. They can do what they like.'

'I'm no' going back to that place,' Alec told his sister stubbornly.

'Yes you are. We both are. Father will get into trouble if we dinna. You heard what she said. It's breaking the law.'

'Will he get the jail?' asked Alec, wide eyed.

'Maybe.'

Morag watched until the coach was out of sight. The girl had been wearing the most beautiful clothes she'd ever seen. And her pretty buttoned boots had been far too good to wear outside on the muddy road.

'It's too late to go back to the school,' said Alec. 'It'll be going-home time when we get there.'

Morag looked up at the sun and nodded. 'We'll go back tomorrow. Let's see if we can find Rob.'

Alec let out a cheer and ran ahead up the bank. Morag followed him, hoping their father had called in at the public house on his way home from work. It would be easier to lie to him if he was drunk.

Two

Dawn broke and the early morning mist on the Forth Estuary began to rise. As it did so, the bridge slowly took shape, as though by magic. The enormous towers seemed to grow upwards from the sea and thrust the clouds aside.

It was a breathtaking sight and Jim Hunter and his two children never tired of it. They had a perfect view from their small camp by the beach.

'Is that porridge no' ready, Morag?' Jim called out, washing his face in a bucket of water.

'It needs a wee minute yet.' She poked at the fire under the pot. 'Alec, can you no' find some dry wood for a change.'

'You try,' he grumbled, still half asleep.

'I bet you a ha'penny I can!' shouted Jim.

'I've no' got a ha'penny,' said Alec.

'No, but I have,' Jim replied. 'Ready, steady, go!'

He ran along the beach and Alec chased after him, scouring the sand for driftwood. Jim picked up a plank with a cry.

'It's wet. Disna count,' Alec told him.

Morag watched them criss-cross the beach like a couple of cavorting dogs and smiled. This was always the best time of day with their father. The pity was that it ended so soon. He had to hurry off to his work, and she and Alec had to drag themselves to school.

'I won!' shouted Alec, running back.

'Och, you cheated,' Jim teased him. 'I saw that bit first.'

'You never,' said Alec.

Jim gave him his ha'penny. 'Mind you share it with Morag.'

'I won it.'

'Never fall out with the cook, son,' said Jim, sitting by the fire with his porridge. 'I did that once, when I was working on the roads. I lost a stone in weight.'

'Is this job better?' Morag asked him.

He shrugged. 'It's still pick and shovel. My hands and back dinna feel no difference. The line to the bridge is through solid rock.'

'I want to go on a train,' said Alec.

'So you will, one day.'

'I'll never have the money.'

'Aye, you will,' said Jim. 'Learn yourself properly at school. Get a good job. No' like me, canna read or write.'

Morag offered him some more porridge. She didn't want him talking about school.

A ship's hooter sounded and the first ferry of the day materialised out of the mist.

'Will there still be ferries?' asked Alec. 'When trains can cross the bridge?'

Jim shook his head. 'Nobody'll use them. The trains will do the crossing in three or four minutes.'

'What's it like, on a train?' Morag asked him.

'Noisy and smoky. And you've to take care no' to get a cinder in your eye from the engine.' He gave a laugh. 'Your granny thought trains were the Devil's work. "It's no' right," she used to say. "Man wisna meant tae gang faster than a horse." She was sure you'd have all the breath blown out of your body. I canna think what she'd say now, with the bridge carrying trains across the sea.'

'Maybe it will blow down in a storm. Like that other one,' said Alec.

'The Tay Bridge?' Jim shook his head again. 'That'll no' happen here.'

'Why no'?'

'Better engineering. Nothing can go wrong. The government's got Board o' Trade Inspectors checking everything.'

Morag caught her breath and crossed her fingers. She hoped against hope Mrs Wright wouldn't do anything. 'They must be awful important,' she said.

'The inspectors?' said Jim with a grin. 'Lassie, round about here, they're more important than the Queen herself.'

'I'm no' going!' shouted Alec.

'You are so,' Morag retorted.

Their father had gone to work and she was lacing up the tent. Alec was supposed to be putting out the fire. In his temper, he kicked at the ashes and burnt his bare foot on an ember. He hopped away, swearing.

'You're no' to say that,' said Morag. 'Serve you right.'

He threw himself down on the grass and put his hands over his ears. Morag went to him. 'You're going, whether you like it or not.' He pretended not to hear and Morag stooped down and shook him. 'Father could lose his job! Be put in the jail! All because of you!'

Alec punched her and ran away. 'You canna tell me what to do!' he cried.

Morag knew her younger brother well enough not to bother replying. She simply marched away and left him. She went along the beach towards the bridge and then along a path that climbed a steep embankment to a narrow cart track. There was no need to glance back to see if Alec was following. She could hear his pathetic wails, together with the cries of the seagulls.

As she walked along, Morag found herself thinking about the girl in the coach. She'd heard that rich people had baths inside their houses and she'd wondered about that. Now she decided it must be true. The girl and her mother had been so clean. As though they'd had a bath that very day. Morag frowned. She didn't like taking her clothes off. That would be the trouble if you had a bath. You'd have to use it. Maybe rich people didn't mind getting undressed. She knew they had things called nightdresses to sleep in, but she couldn't imagine what they looked like.

The track went round to the left, following the edge of a cliff that rose up from the shore. Morag was surprised to find a group of people standing there, looking out to sea.

A man was speaking. 'When I heard yon whistle, I

said to myself, no' another one.'

'I ken,' said his companion. 'You dinna expect it. Now it's nearly finished.'

An old man spat. 'They dinna care. A man's life's nothing to them.'

'I doubt they'll no' be telling the Prince o' Wales how many men it cost, when he opens it.'

Morag realised they were talking about the bridge. Looking out to sea, she saw a steam launch circling under the nearest cantilever.

'The safety boat's searching for him,' said a woman.

'Safety boat,' came the disgusted reply. 'All it can do is pick up the pieces.'

'Aye. From that height, they say you're dead before you hit the water.'

'And then your guts spill out.'

'Away – they dinna!'

'They do so.'

Morag suddenly felt sick. One of the men looked at her. 'You and your big mouth, you've upset the lassie,' he said. 'Dinna fash, lassie. It's no' like that,' he went on to Morag. 'He's blethering.'

It was not only the gruesome details that sickened her. There was also the awful thought that the dead man could be her father. She crossed her fingers and said a silent prayer. But even as she did so, her worry increased. Her mother had told her Bible stories and she'd been sure that God helped people who believed in Him. Morag knew that her father had no time for religion. After his wife's death he'd become bitter. God had let them down.

Could this be God's revenge on him for not believing? Feeling helpless and frightened, Morag watched the small boat. 'What was he doing? The man?' she asked.

The men shrugged and looked blank.

'Was he working on the railway line?'

'Na, na, he'd no' be doing that,' said the old man. 'The line on the bridge has been finished lang syne.'

Another agreed. 'Aye. It's the rails to the bridge they're laying now.'

Morag sighed in relief. It couldn't be her father.

'They've got him!'

The old man was pointing and they all looked at the boat. The crew were leaning over the side, pulling what looked like a black lump out of the sea.

'Did he fall from the bridge?' Alec asked, now by his sister's side. She nodded and felt him clasp her hand.

'They say it's over fifty have lost their lives,' said one of the men.

'I heard sixty,' said another.

Morag and Alec stared at the bridge. The huge structure was like a giant in a story, unaware of the tiny creatures it killed.

'Folk will no' mind that, when they're riding across in their railway carriages,' grumbled the old man.

'I will,' said Morag.

Some of them smiled at the girl in her ragged dress and skimpy shawl.

'And when d'you think the likes o' you will be up there, sitting in style in a railway train?' she was asked and everyone laughed.

Morag and Alec went on their way.

'We've seen a dead man,' he said in a hushed voice.

'Aye,' she said, in her heart thanking God it wasn't her father.

Each of them was dreading what would happen at school, knowing that they would be punished severely for running away. Morag feared the dominie's tawse, but the thing she hated most was not being treated like the other girls. She knew about lepers from the Bible. She was made to feel like one of them. Alec could only think of the pain. The dominie made you put one hand under the other, so the hand he hit didn't bend. Just thinking about it made tears come to his eyes.

'We'll wait till the bell goes before we go into the

yard,' Morag told him in the road outside the school. Passing children mocked them about how hard they would be punished.

The bell rang and they ran into the yard and got into their lines with the others. There was a murmur of surprise from the children. Instead of the dominie, a woman stood before them.

'Mr MacKay has to be away on town council duties today,' she told them. 'My name is Miss Oliphant . . . and there will be no sniggering . . . I shall be in charge. And I warn you, while I am here, only people with clean hands and faces will be allowed in my classroom.'

Together with several others, Morag and Alec were sent to the pump in the yard to wash themselves.

'We'll no' get the tawse!' Alec whispered excitedly.

'Dinna be too sure,' Morag told him. 'And mind you keep quiet.'

Multiplication tables always followed prayers and the children were astonished when Miss Oliphant told them they were going to do drawing. She placed a thistle in a vase on her desk. 'The emblem of Scotland. Your drawing should be tidy. I will not accept anything messy. Take out your slates and begin.'

Miss Oliphant patrolled stiffly between the desks. She was a small woman and made up for her lack of height by holding herself very erect. Her hair and clothes were tightly pinned and tucked and belted. But the biggest difference between her and the dominie was her smell. She gave off the fragrance of lavender. The dominie smelt of his old pipe.

A hand went up.

'Please miss, Morag and Alec Hunter ran out of school yesterday.'

The slates stopped squeaking and there was an expectant silence.

'I see.' Miss Oliphant returned to her desk and picked up the tawse.

Eyes swivelled round to look at Morag and Alec.

'Come out here,' said Miss Oliphant. But she spoke to the boy, not the other two. 'Hold out your hand,' she told him and brought the tawse down hard. 'That's for telling tales. Decent young people do not do that. Return to your seat. And if your thistle is not as neat as ninepence, there will be trouble to pay.'

At playtime Miss Oliphant kept Morag and Alec behind. 'Why did you run away?' she asked.

'Please miss, it wasn't fair,' said Morag. 'They set on us.'

'I see. Has it happened before?'

Morag nodded. 'They just pick on us.'

Miss Oliphant studied them for a moment and then

snapped open her bag. She took out a comb. 'Morag, do you know what this is?' The girl nodded. 'I suspect you haven't got one.' Morag shook her head. 'I'm going to give you this and I want you both to use it. You can start now. After playtime I want to see your hair neat and tidy.'

She left them to get on with it while she wrote sums on the blackboard. They both had tangled mops and neither of them had ever used a comb before. Trying to tug the comb through their hair was difficult and painful. Tears came to their eyes, but they bit their tongues and didn't make a sound. Neither wanted to cause a fuss for Miss Oliphant.

Seeing their red and watering eyes, the other children thought Morag and Alec had been punished. There were sneers and laughs, until Miss Oliphant called the class to order in a stern voice.

'Before you do your sums, we will have Scripture,' she told them. 'Sit up straight with your arms folded. We are going to listen to the word of God. There will be no slouching.' She opened her Bible and read them the story of the Good Samaritan. 'Now, put on your thinking caps. Which of the three men who came along the road was a good neighbour? Hands up.'

'The third one, miss,' came the answer.

'Why?'

'Because he helped the man who was hurt, miss.'

'Correct,' said Miss Oliphant. 'Jesus is telling us to help those less fortunate than ourselves. I want you to remember that. And now, we are going to have a minute's silence. During it, you are to ask yourselves if you have always followed Our Lord's example.'

Morag felt her face turning red. She was sure Miss Oliphant meant the class to think about how she and Alec had been treated. Miss Oliphant was saying Jesus said it was wrong. Morag closed her eyes. The teacher wanted to help them. But she couldn't believe she and Alec could be like anything in the Bible. It didn't seem right.

At hometime Miss Oliphant spoke to the two of them as they were leaving. 'Remember, whatever our station in life, we can be clean and tidy. A good wash and brush-up doesn't cost a penny.'

'I'm no' going to wash every day,' said Alec, as they walked out of the school gates.

Morag put her hand on his arm and they looked about. 'They're no' waiting for us,' she told him.

The road was empty.

'Neither they are,' he said in a whisper. 'We can go to the shop.'

'Whatever for?'

'To spend my ha'penny. We can get two toffee

apples. They're a farthing each. I ken.'

They ran to the shop.

'Stinky tinks!' somebody shouted.

Three

Early on Saturday morning the children went with their father when he left for work. Like all the navvies, he carried his pick and shovel. A man had to work with his own tools. They were like an extra limb and almost as precious.

Alec tried to copy the length of his father's strides. Jim laughed. 'You've a wee bit to grow yet, son,' he told him. 'You'll need to stand on the dung heap.'

'Aye, an' we should leave him there,' said Morag.

'Then you'd have nobody to boss about,' Alec replied, pulling a face at her. 'Can you no' get us another mother?' he asked his father.

'Will you listen to him?' said Jim to Morag. 'You'd think all I had to do was go down to the shop for one.'

'Could you no'?' Alec went on. 'What's wrong wi' wanting a mother?'

Jim slackened his pace, his smile had faded.

Morag felt the change in his mood. 'Stop blethering,' she told Alec.

'I only asked.'

'It's all right, son,' said Jim. 'What do you think, Morag?'

She shrugged. 'I dinna ken.'

'You do so,' cried Alec. 'You've telt me you wished we had a mother.'

'That was different,' said Morag.

'No' it's no',' he persisted.

Morag sighed. 'It's no' only us.' She glanced at her father.

'Would you mind if I got married again?' he asked her.

'I'm no' sure.'

'I wouldna,' said Alec.

Jim ruffled up his son's hair. 'Is that so? Well, it's no' so easy.' His shovel and pick clattered as he altered their position on his shoulder. 'The truth of it is, no' many women are wanting a man wi' two bairns.'

Alec looked at Morag in surprise, but her face didn't change. It wasn't the first time she'd had the feeling that she and Alec made things difficult for their father.

'Would they no' like us, you mean?' asked Alec, in a puzzled voice.

'Looking after a family is hard work,' said Jim.

'We'd help,' said Alec.

'You dinna understand,' Morag told him.

'Shut it,' he snapped at her. 'You always say that.'

Jim looked sideways at his daughter. Like her mother, she kept her thoughts to herself. 'Do you understand?' he asked her. She nodded and carried on walking.

'Most men want a wife,' said Jim. 'It's only natural. I'd like fine to have someone to care for you. Women ken about bairns.'

They reached the village.

'It's pay day,' Jim told them. 'I'll bring you back some sweeties and we'll have that rabbit I caught for our tea.' He left them and joined other men on their way to the new railway cutting.

There was a muffled explosion. Another few yards of rock had been opened up for the navvies to clear.

Morag and Alec stood on a street corner. Both felt unsettled. Neither doubted their father loved them, but it was in a different way from their mother. Maybe he was right and only women knew about children.

They made their way to a row of small houses and knocked on one of the doors. They waited in the yard, beside the wash house and privy. Mrs Bruce was crippled and took a long time answering.

She opened the door slowly and smiled at them. 'Here to earn your Saturday penny,' she said. 'What would I do without you two?'

They got on with their jobs. Morag did Mrs Bruce's washing and Alec collected her groceries from the shop and chopped wood for the fire.

Leaning on her walking stick, Mrs Bruce talked to Morag as she worked in the wash house. 'You're looking a wee bit different, lass. What have you been doing to yourself?'

'I had a wash and combed my hair.'

'Michty me, quite the young lady.'

Morag rubbed the sodden clothes on the washing board and dropped them back in the boiler.

'Mrs Bruce, if my father married again, what would happen?' asked Morag.

'You'd have a step-mother.'

Morag stopped rubbing. 'That's what Cinderella had.'

'Och, it'd no' be as bad as that,' said Mrs Bruce with a laugh.

'She was awful.'

'That was just a story,' Mrs Bruce went on. 'Is your father thinking of getting married?'

'I'm no' sure,' said Morag.

'No' many women would want to live like a tinker

in a tent.'

'Maybe she'd make him live in a house,' said Morag.

Mrs Bruce snorted. 'Then he'd have to mend his ways, if he was to afford the rent.'

Morag nodded reluctantly. 'Drinking must cost a lot of money.'

'You're no' the first to think that, lass. I doubt there's no' a woman in Scotland hasna had the same thought.' Mrs Bruce shook her head. 'It did for my man. It seems they canna do without it.'

Alec came back from the shop. 'There's to be a funeral on Monday,' he said. 'They're going to bury the man who fell off the bridge. We seen him,' he added to Mrs Bruce.

'Poor soul,' she said. 'Nobody said men would have to die. They only talked about how braw it would be.'

'My father says trains will get across in a few minutes,' said Alec.

Mrs Bruce glanced towards the bridge. 'Big as it is, I still canna believe it's there. I get a surprise every morning. Folk cry it the Eighth Wonder o' the World. And to think, it's here on my doorstep.'

'I'm glad,' said Morag. 'It's give father a job.'

'That's what they all say,' said Mrs Bruce. 'As long as you dinna end up a corpse in the sea.' She turned to Alec. 'Put the kettle on the hob. We'll hae a cup o' tea.'

Morag helped Mrs Bruce into the house. 'Thank you, lass. Your pretty hair has set me thinking. Away you go up the stair. You'll find a box on the kist in the wee room. Bring it down to me.'

Upstairs Morag remembered the room they'd lived in before her mother died. It had been just the same, with its sloping ceiling and one small window. It must have been crowded, but it hadn't seemed so to her. She still saw it in her dreams. She sighed. If only they could go back there.

Morag gave the box to Mrs Bruce.

'Open it,' she said.

There were several neatly rolled ribbons inside.

'Choose one for yourself,' Mrs Bruce went on. 'For to tie back your hair. I used to wear them when I was a lass.'

Morag's eye was caught by a crimson ribbon and she took it out. The material was soft and smooth and she let it unroll.

'Can I keep it?' she asked.

'Aye. It's a wee present to you,' said Mrs Bruce. There was a sudden knock on the door and Alec opened it.

A policeman was standing on the step.

'They said in the shop I'd find Jim Hunter's bairns here,' he said.

'What do you want?' said Mrs Bruce.

'I'm to take them up to the railway workings. To the foreman's hut.'

Mrs Bruce gasped and put her hands up to her mouth. 'Has there been an accident?'

The man shrugged. 'I dinna ken. That's my orders.'

Morag gave a cry and Alec ran to her. 'Is it my father?' she asked the policeman.

'I telt you. I dinna ken.'

Mrs Bruce struggled to her feet. 'Off you go, the two of you. I just pray to God it's no' bad.'

The policeman led the children out of the village and up the track to the railway line. Both were upset, but he still kept a close eye on them. The site of the workings was noisy and dusty. They had to thread their way through men and carts and machinery to the hut. Inside, they found the foreman sitting behind a table covered in plans.

'Are you Jim Hunter's bairns?' he asked.

They nodded, frightened of what he was going to tell them. But the man only grunted and opened a door that led into a smaller room. He jerked his head and their father walked in. They ran to him, crying with relief.

Jim Hunter stood in amazement, as his children clutched on to him. 'What's this about?' he asked.

Then he saw the policeman. 'Here, have you two been getting into trouble?' He raised his hand, ready to hit them.

'It's no' that,' said the foreman, sitting at his table. 'I had them brought here.'

'You?' Jim looked at the foreman and then at the policeman. 'Why? What have my bairns got to do with you?'

'I'll tell you,' said the foreman, with a glance at the policeman. 'It's been reported that they're no' being properly looked after.'

'What d'you mean by that?' replied Jim. 'Look at them. They're fit and healthy. They get on fine.'

'There's some folk who wouldna agree with you.'

'Who?' demanded Jim.

'They came to the attention of Mrs Wright.'

'Who does she think . . . '

The foreman interrupted him. 'She's the wife of the Board of Trade Inspector.'

Jim looked baffled. He spoke to the children sharply. 'What have you two been doing?'

'It's no' them, it's you she's complaining about. Letting the bairns run wild and no' go to the school.'

'They go to the school,' Jim protested.

'No' when she seen them,' said the foreman. 'She says they should be taken into care.'

'I look after my bairns!' Jim shouted.

The foreman paused for a moment and sat back in his chair. 'Why d'you no' live in the huts, like the others?'

'I dinna like being crowded in with other folk.'

'You canna bring up a family in a tent. No' if you're a responsible parent.'

Jim glared at the man. 'So that's it, is it?'

'Aye, it is,' said the foreman. 'You're no' capable of looking after your bairns.'

Pushing the children from him, Jim went up to the foreman's table. The policeman stiffened. 'I'm being blamed because they dinna have a mother. I canna help it. I have to be at my work all day. You ken that.'

'Other men in your position pay somebody to keep an eye on their bairns.'

'I dinna want a nosy old wifie . . . '

The foreman cut him off. 'You ken that's no' the reason.' He stood up impatiently. 'Look, it's no' my job to worry about you and your family. I'm paid to get these rails down on time. I'm no' fussed about you. Navvies are ten a penny.'

'No' good ones,' Jim retorted.

'So you think you're a good worker, do you?'

'I ken I am,' said Jim.

The foreman turned his back on him and looked

out of the window at the busy site. 'I dinna like this any more than you. But when I'm telt to do something by the Inspector, I have to jump.'

'I thought it was the bridge he was supposed to inspect,' said Jim.

'That's as maybe,' said the foreman, turning to face him. 'All I ken is this. Either you and your bairns leave North Queensferry . . . '

'Lose my job?'

'I haven't finished,' the foreman went on. 'Or, if you want to keep your job, they'll be taken into care.'

'What does that mean?' asked Jim.

'They'll be put into the Poorhouse and brought up there.'

The children looked at each other and ran to their father.

'Dinna let them!' cried Alec. 'I dinna want to go to no Poorhouse.'

Morag held on to her father's arm. 'We want to stay with you,' she told him.

Jim stared at the foreman. 'They canna take them away . . . '

'They can. According to Mrs Wright, these two have been neglected. She kens the law. And I've been telt. You'll only be kept on here if your bairns are looked after properly.'

'But the Poorhouse?' Jim spoke in a shocked voice.

'What d'you expect?' said the foreman. 'They've no home, no mother. There's no choice.'

'We'll be good,' said Alec in tears. 'Dinna let them . . .'

'So what's it to be?' asked the foreman.

Jim was like a man half asleep. He shook his head, as if he was trying to clear his mind. His children were clinging to him, but he couldn't bear to look at them. He looked at the foreman, his eyes pleading.

'I need my job.'

The children cried out to him.

The foreman nodded. 'I'm sure you do. And you're a good worker. I'll grant you that.'

'No, father . . .' said Morag.

He closed his eyes. 'I do, Morag. I need this job.' He shook his head again. 'Even if I got something else, I'd get less money. We'd be worse off than we are now. I've no choice, lass. No choice.'

When they were taken away, Morag remembered she'd left the ribbon in Mrs Bruce's house. There could be no going back for it now.

Four

'Alec!' Morag let out a cry of surprise.

'Wheest,' he whispered.

'You're no' supposed to be here,' she went on, lowering her voice. 'If they catch you in the female dormitory . . . '

'They'll no'.'

'Quick, get under the bed.' Morag helped him to slide underneath. 'Mind, I'm glad to see you,' she told him, sitting on the bed.

'Me too,' he said. 'Some o' them old men through there scare me. They're no' right in the head, most o' them.'

Morag nodded. 'Like the poor old wifies in here.'

'Morag . . . '

'What is it?'

He was silent for a moment. 'Nothing. I just

wanted to be with you.'

She put her hand down and he took it. 'I'm glad you come,' she said. 'It's a good time. The women are out at their work.'

The two months they had been in the Dunfermline Poorhouse had seemed like years. They saw each other when they went to school, but otherwise they were separated.

'What are you doing?' he asked.

She picked up a half-finished mob-cap. 'Sewing for the poor.'

'Us?' said Alec.

'No. There's supposed to be other folk worse off outside.'

'I canna believe that,' he grumbled.

'Folk wi' nowhere to live,' said Morag.

'They can hae my place here, anytime they want,' Alec told her. 'Are the women noisy, when you're trying to sleep?'

She nodded. 'Aye. I never kent sleeping was such a noisy thing for some people.'

'Me neither.' He gave a snigger. 'In our place they sound like a herd o' swine round a trough.'

'Are you no' supposed to be working?' Morag asked him.

'Aye. Sweeping the yard.'

'You'll get belted if they find you're no' there.'

Alec made a rude noise from under the bed. 'There's some visitor coming. They're no' fussed about me.'

'You canna be sure,' she said, biting off her cotton thread. The tap of a walking stick came down the aisle between the beds. It was Laura, an eleven-year-old blind girl.

'Who are you talking to?' she asked Morag.

'My brother – he's hiding under the bed.'

Laura giggled nervously. 'He's never?'

'I am so,' Alec called out.

'Ssh,' said Morag. 'He sneaked in,' she told Laura, helping the girl to sit by her side.

Laura reached down and touched Alec's hair. He lay rigid as her fingers felt his face. It was a strange sensation, as though a butterfly was trying to find somewhere to land.

'What's it like, being a boy?' she asked him.

'I dinna ken.'

'You must ken something about it,' said Morag.

Alec edged himself out a little way. 'I ken I'm no' a girl,' he said.

'What else?' asked Laura, reaching out and touching his neck and shoulders.

He blew out a breath and thought. 'I want to be

like my father. Strong. He can lift us both up at the same time.'

Laura held the top of his arms. 'Then you'll have to have big muscles.'

Morag smiled. 'They're like knots in cotton now,' she said.

'They're growing,' said Alec. 'What's it like being blind?' he asked Laura.

'Alec . . . !' Morag scolded him.

Laura thought for a moment. 'It's just the way I am.'

'But do you no' want to see?' asked Alec.

'Sometimes. Things I canna touch.'

'Like what?'

Laura shrugged. 'Big things – the sea, the countryside, the bridge Morag's telt me about.'

'It's the biggest in the world,' said Alec. 'It's as long as you can see and as high as the sky.'

'What's the sky like?' asked Laura.

Alec looked at Morag. She put down her sewing and thought. 'Well, you ken it's up above us?'

'Aye.'

'First there's clouds . . '

'What are they like?' said Laura. 'Clouds?'

'Smoke,' said Morag.

'I ken about smoke,' Laura replied. 'I've smelt it.'

'Rain comes from the clouds,' said Alec.

Morag went on. 'But when there's no clouds, you just see the sky. And it's blue. Like the sea is sometimes and people's eyes. And it goes up and up and up . . . '

'To Heaven,' said Alec.

'You canna see Heaven?' Laura said, surprised.

'No, but folk say it's up there,' Morag told her. 'It's in the Bible and that.'

Laura nodded. 'The minister telt me if I'm good, I'll go to Heaven. And when I get there, I'll be able to see.'

'But that's no' till you're dead,' said Alec.

'I ken.'

'We've seen a dead man,' he told her.

'No' really,' said Morag. 'He'd fell off the bridge into the sea.'

'Lots and lots of men have fell off and died,' said Alec.

'They should not've built it then,' Laura responded. 'If God had wanted a bridge there, He'd never've made the Forth so wide.'

The other two looked at her. Oddly, she didn't appear blind. Her eyes were clear and blue, like the sky Morag had tried to describe. It didn't seem possible that she couldn't see you.

They heard the thud of the big front door downstairs and the sound of voices. Laura cocked her head.

'That'll be the Inspector for the Poor. I heard the women say he was coming,' she told them.

Morag jumped up. 'Alec, you'll need to go. Quickly! He mustn't find you here.' She ran to the door and peeped out on to the landing. To her horror, she heard people climbing the stairs. 'They're coming!' she cried.

'What can I do?' pleaded Alec.

The two girls stood close together and he cowered behind them. The voices got to the top of the stairs.

'Listen,' said Laura. 'They're going across the way, into the men's dormitory.'

'I ken,' said Morag, darting to the wooden box at the foot of her bed. She took out her other poorhouse dress. 'Put this on,' she told Alec.

'I canna!'

The girls pulled the dress over his head. Laura buttoned it, while Morag tied a rough apron round his waist.

'My hair!' cried Alec.

Morag put the mob-cap she'd been making on to his head. Laura felt him. 'You're just like a girl,' she said.

'He'll need a job,' said Morag.

'I ken,' said Laura, taking Alec's arm. 'Sit wi' me at the table. I'm making a rag rug. You can pretend you're cutting up the rag into wee bits for me.'

Alec turned a worried face to his sister. 'Morag, I'm scared.'

She adjusted the floppy mob-cap. 'Dinna fash. Now, I'll need to get some sewing for myself.'

Muffled sounds came from across the landing and they waited, holding their breath. There was a commotion when an old man was discovered lying on his bed and was bundled down the stairs to his work.

The dormitory door opened and a bald man marched in angrily. 'It is unforgivable, sir,' he was saying to the cringing Superintendent of the poorhouse. 'The rules laid down by the Committee for the Poor are specific. Nobody skulks in bed in this institution. They work.'

'I inspected the dormitory myself . . . ' the Super-intendent began to say.

The Inspector brushed him aside and stopped by Morag.

'Age?' he asked her.

'Ten, sir.'

'What are you doing?'

'Sewing clothes for poor folk, sir.'

He plucked the material out of her hands, examined it and grunted. 'Work quicker,' he told her.

The Superintendent glowered at Morag. 'Work

quicker,' he repeated pompously.

The Inspector approached the table in the centre of the room. Laura turned her head towards him.

'This girl is impertinent, staring at me like that,' he snapped at the Superintendent.

'She's blind, sir.'

The bald man sniffed. 'That's no excuse.' He picked up Laura's rag rug. 'Do these sell?'

'Oh aye,' said the Superintendent. 'Folk like them on their hearth.'

'Do you have to buy the rags?' asked the Inspector.

'Very rarely. Mostly we get them from the patients who have died at the hospital.'

Alec dropped his scissors. He'd been cutting a tattered pair of trousers into strips. The Inspector regarded him sternly.

'You, girl, you're clumsy,' he told Alec. 'Get back to work immediately.'

Alec kept his head down and made himself pick up the scissors and carry on. He was sure there was the stink of death on the foul rags.

The Superintendent nodded at Laura. 'Not being able to see, making rugs is all she's fit for.'

'I suspect this one is idle,' the Inspector said, pointing at Alec.

'I'll cut down her food if she doesn't improve.' The

Superintendent frowned and looked more closely at Alec. 'When did you come in?' he asked.

'Last night,' said Laura promptly.

'I asked her.'

'She canna speak,' Laura went on. 'She's that upset. Her father fell off the Forth Bridge.'

'Come along, man, I haven't got all day,' said the Inspector.

The Superintendent poked Alec with his finger. 'What's your name?'

'Alice,' squeaked Alec.

The man grunted suspiciously, but hurried after the Inspector. They marched self-importantly round the large room.

'These beds are not properly made and the place needs airing,' the Inspector complained. 'Why are the windows not open?'

The Superintendent pointed at Alec. 'You, open the windows.'

Morag gasped and stood up. 'I'll do it, sir.'

'Get back to your work,' he told her. 'Move yourself, girl,' he ordered Alec.

Reluctantly, Alec got up. The skirt of his dress was too long and he had to clutch it up to move. He found the windows too high to reach. There was a stool under the table and to carry it, he had to let go of his dress. Stumbling, his skirt dragging on the floor, he took the stool to the nearest window. He could feel the Superintendent watching him. Sweat prickled on his forehead and the baggy mob-cap started to slip over his ears.

Normally, he would have hopped up on to the stool in a second, but the skirt either got under his feet, or wrapped itself round his legs. He'd never get up. Angry and frightened at the same time, he tried to jump on to the stool. As he did so, the mob-cap slipped down over his eyes and he fell on to the floor with a clatter. The skirt ended up round his waist, leaving his trousers exposed for all to see.

At supper time, Alec found himself standing on another stool, in the corner of the poorhouse dinner hall. All around him, the inmates were eating their meal. Never before had the thin vegetable broth smelled so good. It reached up to him from the steaming bowls so that he could almost taste it. But his belly was all too aware that he wouldn't be eating any. He was to be allowed only a little bread and water for a whole week. Mocked by some of the others, he bit his tongue and concentrated on not crying.

Later, in bed, he cried his heart out. He lay hugging his knees to his belly, trying to forget his hunger. For once the men's coughing and snoring didn't trouble him, as he struggled to cope with the aching black hole inside himself.

He must have fallen asleep, because he suddenly woke up with a fright. Something was touching his shoulder – tapping him. The room was not totally dark. A little moonlight came through the windows and it glinted on a pair of eyes. They were close to Alec's face. He wanted to yell, but his breath seemed frozen in his body. The urge to leap out of bed was fierce but impossible. He was so terrified he couldn't move.

Alec made out the rest of the face. It was bearded and the mouth had only a few broken stumps of teeth. He was going to be murdered by a madman! In his head he screamed, but not a sound came out. He called for Morag and his father. But his voice was silent. He closed his eyes and prayed.

Tap, tap, tap. He winced and tried to draw away.

A hand slipped behind his back and raised him up. He screwed his eyes tight shut.

'Dinna be feart, son,' said the man. 'I've brung you some food.'

Alec's eyes popped open and as they did, he smelt vegetable broth.

'I saved you a wee bit,' the man went on. 'It's no' hot. But I doubt you'll no' mind that.'

Alec grabbed the bowl and drank greedily.

'There's some bits o' tattie at the bottom.'

Alec picked out the small pieces of vegetable. Now he recognised the old man. He remembered that he'd always been frightened by him and kept out of his way. He'd thought him the ugliest person he'd ever seen.

Five

'Can I play?' Morag asked a group of girls who were skipping. Two of them were turning the rope, while the others ran in to skip.

No one paid any attention to her, and she asked again.

The girls stopped. 'Go away,' one of them told Morag. It was Jean, the school janitor's daughter.

It was a big school and there were separate playgrounds for boys and girls.

Morag went to Laura, who was standing by the wall so that she wouldn't get bumped. 'I kent they'd no' let you,' said Laura, before Morag had even spoken to her.

'You dinna ken everything,' said Morag.

Laura shrugged her shoulders. 'Play wi' me. I can skip.'

'We've no' got a rope,' Morag replied impatiently.

Secretly, she longed to be like the other girls; to join in their chatter and laughter. She and Alec were not bullied, like they had been in the village school. As poorhouse children, they were ignored – like something unpleasant people pretended not to see.

'I dinna mind,' said Laura.

'What?'

'No' playing wi' them.'

'You do really,' Morag told her.

'No I never,' Laura went on. 'I've heard them, blethering away. They just talk rubbish. And to think – they can see.'

Morag looked away from Laura's eyes. She didn't think she'd ever get used to the blind girl's unseeing gaze.

'I hate them,' she said.

Waiting in line to go back inside, she noticed the janitor stacking kindling wood for the school's fires. The bundles of rough timber were tied up with rope.

'Now, who knows the story of the Good Samaritan?' Miss Bell asked the class.

Morag put up her hand. She was sitting with Laura and two other poorhouse children in their place at the back of the class.

'Anyone?' asked Miss Bell, looking round. Morag tried to push her hand even higher.

Another hand went up.

'Yes, Jean?'

'I do, miss.'

'Very well,' said Miss Bell. 'What can you tell us about him – the Samaritan.'

'Please miss, he was good, miss,' said Jean.

'Yes, but how?'

'He did good things, miss.'

'That's right,' said Miss Bell. 'Can you tell us what sort of things, Jean?' The girl didn't answer. 'Anyone?'

Morag was half out of her seat, waving her arm.

Miss Bell shook her head. 'I must say I am disappointed with this class. It seems you are ignorant of one of the most uplifting stories in the Bible.'

Calling out was strictly forbidden, but Morag couldn't help herself. 'Miss, miss, I ken.'

Miss Bell glared at her. 'I will not have misconduct in my class. Morag Hunter, you will stay in during the afternoon break.'

Morag slumped in her seat. She stopped listening to the lesson. She thought about herself and Alec. They had nothing. They didn't own anything, not even their ill-fitting poorhouse clothes. And the only thing they had to look forward to were the brief occasions when they could be together. The others got excited about birthdays, Christmas, and family treats. Were she and her brother going to be forced to miss these things for the rest of their lives? It seemed so. She remembered Mrs Bruce's ribbon and a tear rolled down her cheek.

Morag had to stand in the corner during the afternoon break. She could hear the girls laughing and playing outside. The whirr of their skipping ropes came through the window. Rope. In her mind's eye she saw the bundles of firewood . . . that's how she could get a skipping rope! But it would be tightly knotted. Then she realised she was standing next to the cupboard containing the scissors they sometimes used for cutting out paper shapes. She quickly opened the door and took a pair and put them in her pocket. They were small and blunt, but they might do.

After school Morag met Alec at the gate.

'You'll need to go on by yourself,' she told him. 'I've got something to do.'

'What?' he asked.

'I canna tell you. You could get into trouble.'

'Let me come with you.'

'No.' She sent him on his way and went back into the school yard. It was deserted. She ran to the stack of wood. The rope was perfect for skipping. It was tough and strong, but that also meant it was hard to cut. The school scissors made hardly any impression on it.

Rather than cut, she had to clamp the blades on the rope and twist them round and round.

The sound of crunching boots coming across the yard made her stop. Peeping round the stack she saw the janitor approaching. She gasped. She was going to be discovered! But he halted, as if someone had called him. Then she saw Alec run up to the man and they left the yard together.

Astonished and thankful, Morag knew she had a few more moments. She clamped her fists over the scissors and worked away at the rope. It was coming! Then it snapped. The wood clattered down. She pulled the rope from under it and ran out of the playground.

She wanted to run all the way to the poorhouse, but she had to find Alec. He'd saved her from discovery. What on earth had he said to the janitor?

The rope was about five feet long. She would cut the knot off later. Morag coiled it up and hid it under her dress.

After a few minutes Alec came running up to her, a smile all over his face. 'The jani give me a sweetie,' he said.

'He never?'

'I telt him there was a cat scratching up the vegetables in his garden,' Alec told her.

'You followed me when I telt you not to,' said Morag.

'Aye,' he said, sucking on his sweet. 'I kent you'd be after the rope.'

'How?'

'I seen how you watched the other lassies skipping.'

Morag knew better than to kiss her brother, so she gave him a hug. He hugged her back. But not for too long. It didn't do to be seen hugging your sister.

For once Alec was cheerful when he woke up. It was probably because he still felt good about helping Morag get her rope. He was hungry and hoped somebody wouldn't want their porridge, so that he could get extra.

The men were getting out of their beds with the usual groans and complaints. The ones who had bothered to undress were putting on their clothes. The rest were scratching and yawning. There was an unexpected cry from one of them.

'Tam's away.'

Alec looked at the old man's bed and saw that it was still occupied. What was the man talking about?

Men gathered round Tam's bed and looked down at

him. Alec joined them. He'd been friendly with the old man since he'd sneaked food out for him. Tam was not breathing. His mouth was half open and the skin on his forehead was like marble. With a shiver, Alec saw that he was dead.

He moved away, not wanting so much as another glimpse of the corpse. He sat on his bed. Not only was he in the same room as a dead man, he'd been there when he died. Alec couldn't help picturing himself asleep at the moment of Tam's death. What had happened? Had he called out – tried to get help? Had he known he was going to die, while the others lay snoring?

The Superintendent came in and ordered two of the younger men to carry the body downstairs. As usual, he was irritable and told them that an inmate's death was not to be used as an excuse to be idle. There would be reduced rations for anyone late at his work. Or school, he added to Alec, as he went out.

But Alec remained on his bed. He wanted to tell Tam he was sorry he'd died.

Morag was amazed at how well Laura could skip. Each had an end of the rope and they were skipping side by side.

'Stop, stop – I'm puffed!' cried Morag.

'Me too,' said Laura.

They rested against the yard wall. 'How d'you ken where the rope is?' Morag asked her.

'I can feel it,' said Laura. 'You can hear it and it makes a wee breeze.'

'I couldna do it.'

'You could so. Close your eyes.'

Morag got the rope to the right length and began skipping by herself.

'Are they closed?' called Laura.

'No' yet,' said Morag. 'Here goes, I'm closing them now . . . '

She managed a few twirls, but the rope caught her feet. She giggled and when she opened her eyes, she saw Jean watching her from across the playground.

'You should see the look on Jean's face,' she told Laura.

'She'll no' like us poorhouse rubbish enjoying ourselves,' said Laura. 'It's a braw rope. Let's have a shot together again.'

'Morag Hunter, go into school at once.'

Miss Bell's voice surprised the two girls. They hadn't noticed her coming across the playground. Jean was standing by her side with a smirk on her face.

Morag looked at the teacher. 'Why?' she said.

'Do not be impertinent and give me that rope.'

Morag was belted in front of the whole class. Three strokes of the tawse on each hand. During her punishment she noticed Laura with her fingers in her ears. And she saw that blind people can cry, just the same as everyone else.

During the afternoon Morag was told that her theft would be reported to the police and the Superintendent of the poorhouse. She was then ordered to leave the school. She was to be excluded until the matter was settled.

Upset as she was, there was only one thing Morag wanted to do. Somehow or other she was going to get her own back on Jean.

The girl had heard her father complain about the stolen rope. Seeing Morag skipping, she'd guessed who was responsible and told Miss Bell.

Morag knew the back lane Jean would use to go home. It was raining, but she didn't care. What she had to do was more important than getting wet. She went down the lane and hid in a gateway. Waiting there, she could still feel the pain in her hands from the tawse.

There was also a kind of pain inside her. It came from the feeling that everybody was against her, just because she was poor.

She heard the sudden burst of shouting as the children came out of school. Before long, Jean called goodbye to her friends at the end of the lane and came running along by herself.

Morag stepped out and faced her. Surprised as she was, Jean still managed to give Morag a superior look.

'You clyped on me,' said Morag.

'Because you're a thief. Get out of my way.'

'We're treated like dirt, just 'cause we're from the poorhouse.'

'I'll tell on you again, if you dinna let me by,' said Jean.

'Get by, if that's what you want.'

Jean tried to run round, but Morag threw herself at the girl and they both fell down.

'My dress!' screamed Jean.

They rolled about, clutching each other. Jean was the stronger of the two and Morag knew she wouldn't be able to fight her for long. But Jean's concern for her dress gave Morag an idea. Cart wheels had made ruts in the lane, in which puddles were forming in the rain.

Morag let go of Jean and stood up. Jean attempted to do the same but, when she was halfway up, Morag pushed her and she fell flat into a puddle. Undecided what to do next, Morag shouted at her. 'Now you ken what it's like to be dirt.' Then she ran away, frightened of what she had done.

She found Alec standing in the rain outside the poorhouse.

'I'm no' going back in there,' he told her.

'Neither am I,' she said.

Six

The two children gave up trying to speak to each other. The noise from the huge wooden cart was deafening. They had to cling on as the load of railway sleepers bounced and shuddered over every pothole. The only good thing about their ordeal was that it was taking them away from Dunfermline and the poorhouse.

They had begged food outside a bakers and spent the night hidden in the hay inside a livery stable. At dawn, it had been easy to get a lift from one of the carters heading for the bridge.

Morag and Alec hadn't spoken about their father, but it seemed that going back to North Queensferry was all they could do. They tried not to think about what would happen when they got there. In one respect, their hazardous journey was a help. All they could concentrate on was their survival.

Alec yelled and pointed up at the sky. A small round object was floating in the air over the Forth. A hot air balloon. It had to be. He'd seen a picture of one at school. He stood up excitedly. Morag tugged his shirt to make him sit. But he pulled away from her fussing. At that moment the cart went over a pothole and he fell off.

Morag screamed, but the carter didn't hear her at the front. She climbed over the tailgate and dropped down on to the road as the cart lumbered on. Getting up, she hurried back to Alec, who had fallen into the ditch at the side of the road. He was lying very still and there was blood on his head. She cradled his head and spoke to him, but he was unconscious. Frightened, she looked around. What could she do? She had to have help.

She heard a horse and rider approaching. Quickly, she bundled up her shawl and put it under Alec's head. The galloping horseman paid no attention to her waves. She waited and a gig came along. But its occupants dismissed her as yet another beggar and carried on.

Crying, Morag went back to Alec. She eased his body to make him comfortable. Nervously, she felt his heart. Its beat reassured her a little, but she was desperate. She could hardly see for the tears in her eyes.

She became aware of a shadow. A woman was standing on the road, looking down at them. Her clothes were rough and she was smoking a small clay pipe.

'Is he hurt?' she said.

'Aye, he's dunted his head,' Morag told her.

The woman took her pipe out of her mouth and spat. She rummaged in the handcart beside her and found some dark green leaves. 'Give him a whiff o' these,' she said. 'Hold them under his neb.'

Morag did as she was told and seconds later Alec was trying to brush them away from his nose. His eyes opened and he saw the woman. His body twitched.

'What about his head?' Morag asked. 'It's bleeding.'

'Come wi' me. I'll sort it.'

They helped Alec up and the woman cleared a space for him to sit on her cart. The movement of the bags and boxes released a strange mixture of smells. Some as pleasant as perfume, others like the earth. Alec sat trying not to touch anything as he was wheeled along.

The woman led them off the road to a tinker encampment in a strip of woodland between two fields. A man and young boy were squatting down making clothes pegs. Beside them was the family's bender, a tent made over a frame of saplings. There were several cats and one of them jumped up on to the cart and rubbed itself against Alec.

The woman spoke to the boy in words Morag didn't understand. He went away into the trees.

They sat Alec down by the camp fire and the cat settled itself on his lap. The man watched him without speaking.

'What do they cry you?' the woman asked Alec. He told her in a whisper. She nodded, examining the wound. 'You've had a fell dunt Alec.' She put one hand behind his neck and gently rubbed his thumb with her other hand. He stiffened at her touch, but his body soon relaxed.

Morag looked on uneasily. The same heady mixture of smells hung over the campsite. She was sure they were coming from a collection of leaves and roots laid out by the bender. The tinkers must pick them. Why? The thought began to grow in Morag's mind that the woman might be a witch. Witches captured children.

The boy came back, his hands cupped in front of him. His mother held open her own hands and he gently tipped something into them.

'Cobwebs,' said the woman, answering Morag's

gaze. 'Hold your head still, Alec. It'll no' hurt.' With great care she covered his wound with the cobwebs. 'Now lie back.' Alec did so and she spoke to the boy, who brought her some moss. She also placed this over the wound. 'Sleep, Alec,' she said, and his eyes closed.

'Cut,' said the boy, standing in a thicket and cutting down a slim branch. 'Strip.' He ran his knife along its length and stripped off the bark.

Morag and Alec watched him, fascinated, as he showed them how to make pegs. He had very few words of English and they'd discovered his father had none.

It was late afternoon and the smell of cooking came from the distant camp fire. The boy was shy, but he seemed to enjoy being with them. He laughed when the newly stripped wood slipped in their hands. But he was eager to show them how to handle it properly. Just after they had each succeeded in making a peg, his mother called and he left them.

'I think she might be a witch,' said Morag, as soon as they were alone. Alec's hand shot up to his wound. 'Dinna touch it!' she cried, pulling his hand down. She looked at the wound herself. The cobwebs had disappeared and a scab was starting to form.

'I'm no' going to stay wi' no witch . . . ' Alec started to say.

'She's cooking tea,' said Morag.

They looked at each other. Both were starving and the smell was almost too much to bear.

'We could jinx off after we've eaten,' he suggested.

Morag frowned. 'Maybe there's good witches,' she said. 'Why would she make you better if she was bad?'

'To trick us.'

She shook her head. 'Witches dinna have children of their own.'

'She could've stole him.'

Morag could think of no answer to that. She thought about the cats. Witches had cats – but only one black one. 'They could just be tinks,' she said. 'That's what they look like. I think she collects they leaves and plants and sells them.'

'Aye, for spells,' said Alec.

The woman called them and on their way to the camp they saw the boy. He was in a nearby field, milking a cow.

They were given spoons and the five sat round a large pot of stew that had been lifted off the fire. Alec bent forward to put his spoon in, but the woman halted him. She looked at the man and he spoke some words in their own language. Then she nodded and they began the meal.

The stew was delicious. Morag and Alec had never tasted anything like it before. Morag recognised some of the vegetables in it, but they had an unusual flavour. She was glad everybody was eating the same. It meant that if the woman was a witch, at least she wasn't trying to poison them. When the pot was empty, they drank the fresh creamy milk the boy had brought.

'I seen a balloon,' said Alec.

'That's how he fell off the cart,' Morag said.

The woman nodded. 'I seen it too. I canna see the sense o' it.' She lit her pipe.

'It must be braw, being up in the air,' Alec went on.

'The air's for birds,' said the woman. 'Why do folk want to go up where there's nothing, when there's so much for them here on the ground?'

The man and the boy began playing a game. They picked dandelion clocks and took turns in blowing their seeds over the fire. The hot air shot the seeds upwards and the winner was the one who got highest.

'You,' said the boy to Morag and Alec, who joined in the game.

The man sat down and began humming and clapping his hands. The woman beat time with her pipe and then started singing in their language.

Listening to them, Morag had a strange feeling. It was as though their music belonged only to that place. Like the mysterious smells.

The boy stopped still. 'Watch,' he told them, as the song went on. He poured some milk into a wooden platter and put it down a few feet away from the fire. 'Wait,' he said. They watched the platter, not knowing what to expect. After a few minutes there was a rustle in the undergrowth and a hedgehog appeared. It snuffled its small, pig-like nose, and went to the milk and began to drink.

The dusk was giving way to darkness and the man built up the fire. Then he and the boy curled up by it and went to sleep, just as the cats had done.

The woman nodded towards the bender. 'You can sleep in there,' she told Morag and Alec.

'Should they no' be in there?' asked Morag.

'They want you to have it.'

Morag looked at Alec. She could see he was tired and had given up the idea of running off. 'Thank you for helping us,' she said. 'We've got nothing we can give you.'

A smile crossed the woman's face. 'I ken. Where were you going?'

Morag told her. 'We canna think o' nowhere else.'

The woman took hold of Morag's hands and said

something in her own language.

'What did you say?' Morag asked.

'It's what we say to bring folk good luck.' She squeezed the girl's hands and let them go.

'What are they – all your leaves and roots?' said Morag.

'Leaves and roots,' she answered.

'Are they no' special?'

'Only when you ken what to do wi' them. Old wifies buy them from me because they think I make them special. They dinna say so, but they're wanting something magic. Like most folk.' She gave a chuckle. 'Everybody kent what I ken, once.'

'How did they forget?'

'Because folk aye think new things are better,' said the woman. 'I have my doubts about that.'

'Like the balloon?'

'Aye.'

'The bridge is better,' said Alec sleepily.

'No' for me, it's no',' said the woman.

'Folk cry it the Eighth Wonder of the World,' he said, remembering what Mrs Bruce had told them.

'I'll tell you what's wonderful, Alec,' she said, leading him into the bender and gently lying him down. 'You, your sister, yon wee hedgehog, animals, the birds in the sky. The trees and plants. The magic of things growing.' She brushed the hair from his face as he fell asleep. 'And they'll still be here when your bridge has rotted away.'

Seven

The next day the tinker woman gave them some oatmeal and saw them on their way. 'Beware o' folk who live in houses,' she told them. Muttering something in her own language, she disappeared amongst the trees.

On a signpost they saw that North Queensferry was only four miles away.

'Will our father send us back?' said Alec.

Morag sighed. 'I dinna ken. Maybe.'

'I'll no' go, if he does.'

'You'll have to.'

'I'll run away and make clothes pegs,' he said.

She smiled at him. 'Then you'd be a real tinker. Folk have been crying us tinks for long enough.'

'I like tinkers.'

'They're better than a lot o' folk I can think of.'

Alec walked on. He seemed to be deep in thought. 'If he lets us stay, we'll have to go back to that school.'

'It might be different now.'

'No' wi' that dominie,' said Alec firmly. 'If he's there, I'll no' go.'

Morag laughed. 'To listen to you, you're no' going to go nowhere,' she said. 'We can only wait and see what happens.'

Going round a bend in the deserted road, they heard the sound of singing. It grew louder and they looked to see where it was coming from.

'See, there . . . ' Alec pointed at a young man on top of a hillock in a field. He was singing and dancing a jig. 'He must be a daftie,' said Alec.

The young man waved when he saw them and ran down the slope.

'Come on, come on, you're just in time,' he said breathlessly. They looked at him suspiciously. 'Hurry up!' he cried.

'What for?' asked Morag.

He threw up his arms in the air. 'The most important day in the history of the world!' he shouted, running back up the slope.

His excitement was infectious. The two children exchanged glances and chased after him. At the top there was a grand view of the whole of the Forth

Bridge. The young man was dancing again and he weaved in and out between the children.

'Is it to do with the bridge?' said Alec.

The young man stopped still. 'D'you no' ken? The first train's going across today.'

'Is the bridge open then?' Morag asked him.

'No. No' yet,' he said. 'This is a test train, loaded to double its weight. It's to test the strength o' the bridge's structure. I've walked from Glasgow to see it. If it works, it'll be an engineering miracle. And we'll be the first to see it.'

'How d'you ken about it?' said Alec.

'I'm an engineer,' the young man said proudly. 'I've just finished my apprenticeship. One day I'm going to build something great.' He pointed at the bridge enthusiastically. 'Look at it. They had to develop and cast special steel. Rivet girders at impossible angles. Working under the sea.'

'Are you going to make a bridge?' Alec asked him.

He scratched his head thoughtfully. 'Bridges take a long time. I was thinking I'd have a shot at making a flying machine.'

'A balloon?'

He waved his hand dismissively. 'Balloons are no' flying machines!'

'They go up in the sky,' said Morag.

'They're only full of hot air,' he went on. 'Like the folk who go up in them. My flying machine will have an engine in it. So you can fly where you want to go.'

They gazed at him, sure he was mad.

'One day flying machines will be as common as trains.'

Faintly, but clearly, they heard the distant whistle of a railway engine. They peered at the bridge.

'It's starting! It's starting!' cried the young man.

Soon they saw small puffs of smoke coming from the southern end of the bridge. They strained their ears and could just hear the snort of the engine, struggling with its heavy load.

'Look!'

The tiny train came into view.

'It's going so slowly,' said Morag.

'Of course it is,' said the young man. 'In case something goes wrong. They dinna ken if the structure is sound yet. It could collapse.'

Some of the vessels sailing on the Forth sounded their hooters. The children and the young man fell silent, willing the train to get across safely. They felt like they could help it. There was also the feeling that something very special was happening.

'Go on, go on!' Alec burst out.

When the train reached the viaduct at the northern

end of the bridge, the three of them jumped in the air and cheered. They danced a wild highland fling in celebration and then fell down exhausted.

'It works!' said the young man, gasping for breath.

'I kent it would,' said Alec.

Morag wiped the sweat off her face. 'Aye, but it's no' for the likes of us,' she told the young man. 'It's a braw bridge. But it's for folk wi' money. No' Alec and me.'

'Blethers!' he snorted, grabbing her hands and pulling her up for another dance. 'The world and his wife will be crossing before long.'

'God save us!' said Morag, clutching at Alec. She'd seen the village policeman. He was walking up the street towards them.

'What'll we do?' hissed Alec.

'Run!'

She took his hand and they ran across the street and down a close between the houses.

'He's seen us!'

They ran along a back alley with the man puffing after them.

'Up here.' Morag led Alec up another close to the main street. They came out by the church. The hall beside the church was open. They ran inside. Long tables were laid with tablecloths and cutlery, ready for a meal. Both had the same idea and they dived under one of the tables. Voices and the clatter of plates came from the small kitchen.

The tread of heavy boots rattled the cutlery. They marched the length of the hall to the kitchen. A man's voice interrupted the others. Morag and Alec held hands, not daring to breathe. Feet walked round the hall.

'There's no bairns in here,' said a woman.

'I was sure I seen them come in,' the policeman replied.

'You've been on the whisky,' said a second woman. 'Like all the other men. Thank the Lord we dinna get many public holidays.'

'There's no fear o' that. I doubt we'll never see another bridge finished.'

The policeman clumped out, leaving the women laughing.

'Is that no' typical?' complained one. 'Chasing bairns, when he should be controlling they drunken navvies.'

'Shall I put the cold ham out?'

'Aye. A plateful on each table. They can help themselves.'

As soon as they heard the plates being banged down, Morag and Alec felt hungry. There was an appetising smell of cooking coming from the kitchen.

When the hall was silent again, Alec lifted the tablecloth and looked around. It was clear. The women were back in the kitchen. He sneaked out quickly, snatched a plate of ham and hid underneath again.

'You'll get us into trouble,' Morag whispered.

'I'm hungry,' he said, eating a slice of ham. 'It's braw.'

Morag joined him and they chewed away greedily.

Footsteps came from the kitchen. 'I'll put the bread out,' said the woman. More plates were set down. 'Jean, you're a plate o' ham short,' she called.

'No, I'm no', said the other, coming in. 'I put . . . Jings, you're right. I was sure I'd done them all. Just a minute, that tablecloth's squint . . . '

Two pairs of feet approached the children's table. They froze. Alec held on to the plate. But it was greasy and he was nervous. His fingers slipped and the plate fell on the floor.

The tablecloth was immediately turned back.

'Well!' cried the woman. 'He was right. They *are* here.'

'We were hungry,' said Alec. 'We've had nothing to eat for two days.'

'Why no'?' demanded one of the women.

Morag took a deep breath. She could feel her heart beating. 'Our mother give us a basketful o' pegs to sell. But a man robbed them off of us.'

'Tinks,' said the woman with a sniff.

'Aye,' said her companion. 'Look at the state o' them.'

'We're frightened to go back,' said Morag.

'Because we didna get her no money,' added Alec.

They were taken into the kitchen, sat on a bench and given some food. The women were kind, but it was clear they intended to tell the policeman. Morag and Alec were tense. They'd got to escape.

Morag spoke to the women. 'There's our wee brother.'

'Another one?' they exclaimed in surprise.

'Aye. He's under one of the other tables.'

Chattering indignantly, the women went back into the hall. As soon as they were alone, Morag and Alec dashed out of the back door.

The main street was crowded. Everyone was outside for the holiday. A brass band was playing by the harbour and people were dancing. Some of the villagers were organising sports and games for the children.

In front of one of the pubs a crowd of men were

shouting and cheering. A fight was going on. Alec
wanted to watch.

'No,' said Morag. 'It's too risky. We could get
caught.'

But the temptation was too strong for Alec and he
left her and wormed into the spectators.

The two men were too drunk to fight properly.
They staggered round each other, flinging punches
that missed more often than hit. Alec enjoyed himself,
joining in the cheers and boos. Before long the
fighters were slumped in each other's arms and the
crowd began to thin out. Then Alec saw the
policeman. He was holding Morag by the arm.

Immediately feeling guilty for what he'd done, Alec
panicked. He went to the two reeling fighters and
yelled in their ears.

'He's attacking my sister!'

The two men shook their fuddled heads and
blinked at him. He shouted at them again. Suddenly
they came to life and leapt at the policeman with a
roar. The poor man yelped and let Morag go as they
fell on him.

Morag skipped out of the way and she and Alec ran
out of the village.

They found themselves on the track leading up to
the railway workings. Both of them remembered it

from the terrible day they'd been sent to the poorhouse. But the foreman's hut was no longer there. Instead, a railway station was being built on the site. Even though it was not completed, the building looked impressive. The children stood staring at it.

'They must've finished the railway line,' said Morag.

As she spoke, they had the same thought.

'What about our father?' said Alec.

Morag was at a loss. She didn't want to believe what she was thinking. She hated the smell of fresh timber and paint coming from the station.

'I dinna ken,' she said, shaking her head.

Without speaking, they skirted the village and made their way to their father's campsite.

When they got there, his tent was nowhere to be seen.

Eight

It was only because Alec was crying that Morag managed to hold back her own tears. She wanted to sob her heart out. But instead she comforted her brother.

'What can we do?' he said.

'Go to the burn.'

'Why?'

'For to wash our faces,' she told him, leading the way.

'I'm no' going to wash my face,' he protested angrily.

'D'you want folk to see you've been greetin'?' asked Morag.

He scowled, but followed her. The cold water made Morag shiver and she rubbed her face hard. If only they could wash away their bad luck. The tinker woman's spell, or whatever it was, had made no difference at all. Things seemed to be worse than before.

Morag shook her head. Her hair had got wet and she pulled it back. She needed something to tie it. The thought gave her a sudden idea.

'I ken what we can do. We can go to see Mrs Bruce.'

'She'll have got somebody else to do her jobs,' said Alec, drying his face on his shirt.

'But she would help us,' said Morag. 'She might even ken where our father is.'

They could hear singing and laughter as they walked back to the village. It seemed they were the only ones not enjoying themselves. A merry-go-round had been erected and it spun round to the music of a barrel organ. Morag and Alec stopped to watch. It was the most colourful thing they'd ever seen, with its brightly painted horses.

'It's no' fair,' said Alec, tears in his eyes again. 'We never get nothing.'

Morag remained silent. How often she wished she could complain and burst into tears, rather than always having to care for her brother. That wasn't fair, either – cheering him up, when she was sick at heart herself.

And then, unexpectedly, she remembered Laura. If she was here, she wouldn't be able to see the colour and the spectacle. But Morag knew she would still be excited. Laura was far more deprived than either of them, and yet she didn't complain. The thought made Morag feel ashamed. She turned to Alec and spoke to him sharply.

'Stop greetin'. I'm sick o' you and your tears.' She set off and left him.

Hurt by her rough tone, he followed. Wisely, he stopped crying and didn't protest.

The smell of beer and tobacco smoke came wafting out of an open pub door. Women were shrieking with laughter and folk were singing. There was also the sound of furniture being knocked about. Suddenly two men came reeling out of the door, fighting.

Morag took a firm hold of Alec and led him away.

'Dinna, Morag – I think it's father!' he shouted.

They looked at the men and saw Jim Hunter. He seemed to be fighting for his life. His opponent was both taller and heavier, and lashing out with vicious punches. Morag and Alec were horrified at what was happening.

'Can we no' stop it?' cried Alec.

People were spilling out of the pub and gathering round the fighters. There were cheers when Jim took a blow to the head. 'Give him another one!' somebody yelled.

'Aye, finish him off!' shouted a drunken woman.

'Shut your face!' Morag screamed at her.

The woman took a swing at Morag, but she ducked and jabbed the woman with her elbow.

Morag and Alec dodged around the outside of the crowd.

A large cry went up. Jim was down on the ground. The big man raised his foot to kick him, but Jim managed to grab his boot and topple him over. Another cry, as the two grappled together on the ground.

'Father's bleeding,' said Alec. 'He's hurt.'

The two men rolled and crashed into a wheelbarrow.

'That's father's barrow,' said Morag.

The men let go of each other and were on their feet again. The big man charged, simply using his weight to crash into Jim and wind him. Jim staggered. His opponent lined up a punch.

'You fat pig!' Alec yelled.

Both Jim and the other man hesitated at the sound of Alec's voice.

'Alec!' cried Jim.

'Why you wee . . . ' The big man turned to hit

Alec, but Jim punched him in the belly.

'It's me you're fighting – you fat pig!' shouted Jim. The man roared and the crowd urged him on. 'Flatten him, Tam.'

'Give him the boot.'

'Break his neck.'

Jim skipped around on his toes, but the space was getting smaller. The big man's friends were urging the crowd forward to limit Jim's room.

Without a second thought, Morag and Alec thrust themselves in front of the crowd and tried to move them back. They screamed and clawed like wildcats.

'Give them room, give them room!'

The surprise of their sudden onslaught had an effect. People did step back, treading on those behind and creating angry confusion. Hands grabbed at the children and eventually they were dragged through the crowd.

They heard a punch and a cheer. Jim had been hit. He was almost out on his feet.

Morag and Alec were desperate and helpless.

There was a crash. The swaying crowd had backed into the wheelbarrow and knocked it over. Jim's tent fell out and his pots and pans clattered on the ground. The children ran to save the things. Morag saw the tent's guy-rope lying in the mud. She picked it up and tugged Alec's shirt. He nodded, knowing what she meant.

Heads down, they burrowed through the throng of bodies. At the front of the crowd Alec held on tight to one end of the rope, while Morag took the other and dashed into the fight. The men were separated. Jim could hardly stand and the big man was winding up to deliver the final blow. Morag raced round and round Jim's opponent, wrapping the rope around his legs. In seconds he was trussed and couldn't move. He yelled and waved his arms, and then fell over with a heavy clump on the ground.

For a moment the crowd looked on in silence. Everyone was amazed. No one had ever seen anything like it before. There was no doubting the children's bravery – but above all, they'd been funny. A sudden burst of laughter and cheering broke out. Morag and Alec were hoisted high in the air and showered with money and sweets. What a way to end a fight!

Drifting back into the pub, the spectators were quite sure they'd never been better entertained. The fight beat all the other holiday side-shows put together. Folk would be talking about it for years to come.

Alec had got a fire going and was heating up three pies for their meal. He also had a pot of water bubbling to make tea.

Jim was sitting outside the tent and Morag was putting cobwebs over a cut on his face.

'You're a wee tinker,' he told her. 'What else did that woman learn you?'

'How to make pegs,' called Alec.

Jim eased his body. Every bit of it felt bruised, or aching. 'I still canna believe it,' he said. 'There I was, on my way to get you, and then I seen you in the crowd.'

'Who was that man?' asked Morag. 'The one you were fighting?'

Jim grunted. 'He'd been paid off, the muckle lump.'

'Lost his job?' said Alec.

'Aye. Most of the navvies have.'

'What about you?' said Morag.

Jim grinned. 'I've got another job. That's what was eating him. He was jealous. I was having a wee drink before setting out for Dunfermline. He comes up, starts calling me a dirty tink. He was out for a fight.' He shook his head. 'Mind, I'm glad you come. There was no way I could've gone on much longer.'

Morag went to the bucket and washed her hands.

She glanced at Alec. Was he thinking the same thing? Something about his quietness suggested that he was. Morag stood up and spoke to their father.

'Were you really coming to get us?' she asked him.

Jim let out a breath and nodded. 'Aye, lass, I was. I ken what you're thinking. But it's the truth. I ken I've no' been much of a father to you. But I had no choice about the poorhouse.'

'I'm no' going back there,' said Alec defiantly.

'You never sent us no letter, or nothing, when we were there,' Morag told Jim.

'You ken I canna write.'

'If you were coming to get us, why were you in the pub?' Morag asked.

'I telt you,' said Jim. 'I was having a wee drink – to celebrate getting my new job. That's how I was able to go and get you back. I'll have more money now. We can live together again.'

Morag and Alec looked at each other, but neither spoke.

'Trust me, I'm telling you the truth,' Jim went on. 'To start with, this is the last night you'll sleep in this tent. Tomorrow we're moving into a house. I'm renting Mrs Bruce's top two rooms for us.'

His children gazed at him, hardly daring to believe their ears.

'Is your job here?' said Alec slowly.

'Aye. On the bridge.'

'But it's finished,' Morag said.

'That's why!' Jim cried, getting to his feet. Wincing with pain he went to them by the fire. 'You're no' going to believe this neither, but it's the truth. The bridge has to be painted. There's a team of twenty-eight painters – and I'm one o' them.'

Alec gasped. 'You have to paint it?'

'So's the metal disna rust,' said Jim.

'Just think, Morag,' Alec said to her, his eyes gleaming.

She made no movement. Her own eyes were filling with tears. She felt them trickling down her face, but she didn't try to stop them. A home, at last. And with the kindly Mrs Bruce. She tried to smile, but found herself weeping.

Jim Hunter put his arm round his daughter and comforted her.

Alec looked at his elder sister and shook his head. 'Is that no' like a lassie. Greetin'!' He ran down to the beach. 'What happens when you finish painting the bridge?' he called.

'It'll never be finished,' Jim shouted.

Alec turned and walked back. 'You mean you'll go on forever?' he asked in astonishment.

Jim nodded, and the three of them looked in wonder at the giant cantilevers striding across the Firth of Forth.

Postscript

Five thousand men worked day and night for seven years to complete the Forth Rail Bridge and its approaches. They used 51,000 tons of steel and 5,000,000 rivets. The highest part of the bridge is 110 metres and the deepest part is 28 metres below water.

There are two spans of 521 metres and two of 207 metres, and the overall length is 2.4 kilometres.

The bridge was open for rail traffic on 4 March 1890. Fifty-seven men lost their lives during its construction.